The Jumblies

Edward Lear

Illustrated by
Ian Beck

DOUBLEDAY

They went to sea in a Sieve, they did,

In a Sieve they went to sea;

In spite of all their friends could say,

On a winter's morn, on a stormy day,

In a Sieve they went to sea!

TRANSWORLD PUBLISHERS
61-63 Uxbridge Rd, London W5 5SA
A division of The Random House Group Ltd

RANDOM HOUSE AUSTRALIA (PTY) LTD
20 Alfred Street, Milsons Point, Sydney,
New South Wales 2061, Australia

RANDOM HOUSE NEW ZEALAND LTD
18 Poland Road, Glenfield, Auckland 10, New Zealand

RANDOM HOUSE (PTY) LTD
Endulini, 5A Jubilee Road, Parktown 2193, South Africa

Published in 2001 by Doubleday
a division of Transworld Publishers

1 3 5 7 9 10 8 6 4 2

Copyright © Ian Beck 2001
Designed by Ian Butterworth
The right of Ian Beck to be identified as the Illustrator
of this work has been asserted in accordance with
the Copyright, Designs and Patents Act 1988

A catalogue record for this book is available
from the British Library

ISBN 0 385 60117 4

And when the Sieve turned round and round,

And everyone cried, "You'll all be drowned!"

They called aloud, "Our Sieve ain't big,

But we don't care a button! We don't care a fig!

In a Sieve we'll go to sea!"

But we don't care a button!

We don't care a fig!

Far and few, far and few,
Are the lands where the Jumblies live;
Their heads are green, and their hands are blue,
And they went to sea in a Sieve.

They sailed away in a Sieve, they did,

In a Sieve they sailed so fast,

With only a beautiful pea-green veil

Tied with a riband by way of a sail,

To a small tobacco-pipe mast;

And everyone said, who saw them go,

"O won't they be soon upset, you know!

For the sky is dark, and the voyage is long,

And happen what may, it's extremely wrong

In a Sieve to sail so fast!"

Far and few, far and few,
Are the lands where the Jumblies live;
Their heads are green, and their hands are blue,
And they went to sea in a Sieve.

The water it soon came in, it did,

The water it soon came in;

So to keep them dry, they wrapped their feet

In a pinky paper all folded neat,

And they fastened it down with a pin.

And they passed the night in a crockery-jar,
    And each of them said, "How wise we are!
Though the sky be dark, and the voyage be long,
    Yet we never can think we were rash or wrong,
While round in our Sieve we spin!"

Far and few, far and few,
Are the lands where the Jumblies live;
Their heads are green, and their hands are blue,
And they went to sea in a Sieve.

And all night long they sailed away;
 And when the sun went down,
They whistled and warbled a moony song
 To the echoing sound of a coppery gong,
In the shade of the mountains brown.

"O Timballo! How happy we are,

   When we live in a Sieve and a crockery-jar,

And all night long in the moonlight pale,

   We sail away with a pea-green sail,

In the shade of the mountains brown!"

O Timballo! How happy we are

Far and Few, Far and Few,
Are the lands where the Jumblies live;
Their heads are green, and their hands are blue,
And they went to sea in a Sieve.

They sailed to the Western Sea, they did,
  To a land all covered with trees,
And they bought an Owl, and a useful Cart,
  And a pound of Rice, and a Cranberry Tart,
And a hive of silvery Bees.

Aɴᴅ they bought a Pig, and some green Jack-daws,

And a lovely Monkey with lollipop paws,

And forty bottles of Ring-Bo-Ree,

And no end of Stilton Cheese.

Far and few, far and few,
Are the lands where the Jumblies live;
Their heads are green, and their hands are blue,
And they went to sea in a Sieve.

And in twenty years they all came back,

    In twenty years or more,

And everyone said, "How tall they've grown!

    For they've been to the Lakes, and the Torrible Zone,

And the hills of the Chankly Bore";

And they drank their health, and gave them a feast

    Of dumplings made of beautiful yeast;

And everyone said, "If we only live,

    We too will go to sea in a Sieve,

To the hills of the Chankly Bore!"

Far and few, far and few,
Are the lands where the Jumblies live;
Their heads are green, and their hands are blue,
And they went to sea in a Sieve.

We too will go to sea in a Sieve...

The Hills of the Chankley Bore

The Western Sea

A Land All Covered in Trees